MUMMY NEVER TOLD ME

Babette Cole

RED FOX

Mummy never told me that life
is full of little secrets.

Like, what is my
tummy button
for . . .

and how did it get there?

Why is Mummy so busy
that she has no time for me?

Why must I go to school . . .

when Mummy was expelled from hers?

What does the tooth fairy

really look like?

Mummy never told me that
boys are different from girls . . .

or that
it's hard
to tell

the grown-up
ones apart!

Why do
grown-ups
have hair
in their
ears,

and up their
nostrils,

but sometimes
none on their
heads?

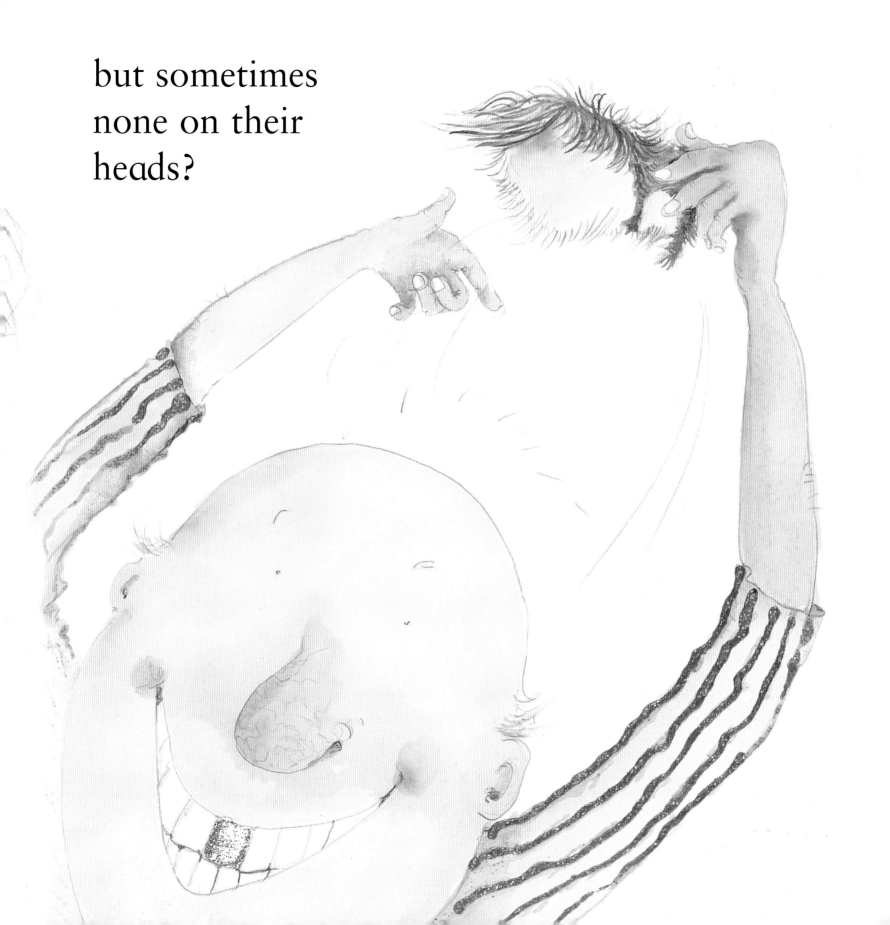

Doctors can help them
choose a new nose.

But they don't tell you what
to do with the old ones!

She didn't tell me why
some grown-ups go to sleep
with their teeth in a jar beside them,

or why they
spend so long
in the bathroom!

Why do Mummy and Daddy

lock me out of their bedroom?

BOING

Where do they go

at night?

Where do mummies and daddies
who can't have babies get one from?

How can you
hate someone . . .

and love them
at the same
time?

Why do some women prefer to
fall in love with other women . . .

and some men
with other men?

But I'm not worried.
She'll tell me when the time comes!

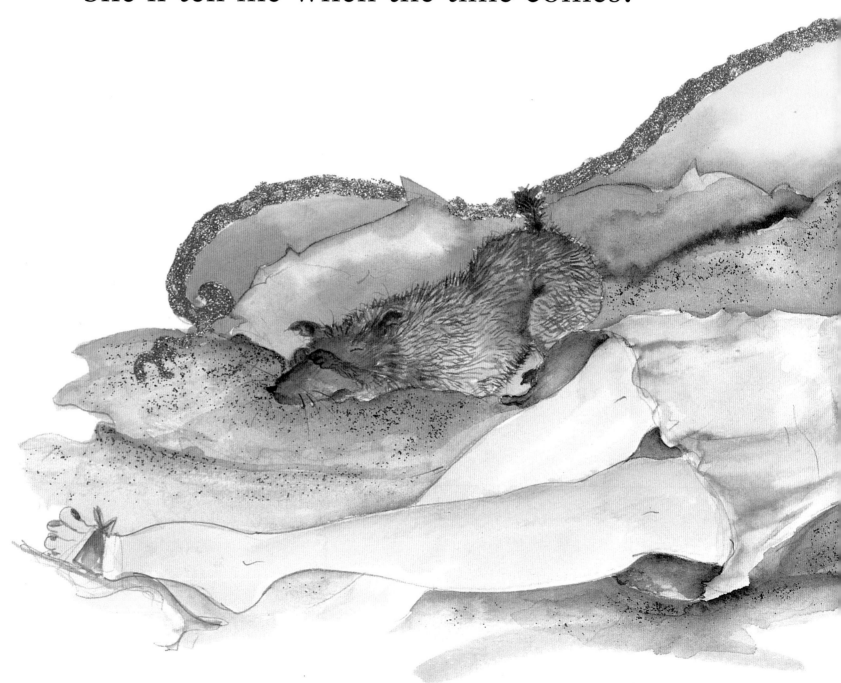

To Boo

MUMMY NEVER TOLD ME
A RED FOX BOOK 978 0 09 940713 3

First published in Great Britain by Jonathan Cape,
an imprint of Random House Children's Books

Jonathan Cape edition published 2003
Red Fox edition published 2004

5 7 9 10 8 6

Copyright © Babette Cole, 2003

Red Fox Books are published by RANDOM HOUSE CHILDREN'S BOOKS
61–63 Uxbridge Road, London W5 5SA
Addresses for companies within The Random
House Group Limited can be found at:
www.randomhouse.co.uk/offices.htm

THE RANDOM HOUSE GROUP Limited Reg. No. 954009
www.kidsatrandomhouse.co.uk
www.babette-cole.com

A CIP catalogue record for this book is available from the British Library

Printed in Singapore